Able Lieder hasn't seen his mate in six days, but he can't do anything about it. He knows the guard—Olson—doesn't understand why he feels drawn to him, bringing him treats and talking sweetly to him. He can't explain it to him, either, since the scientists are keeping him in cat form. When Able overhears the scientists talking about an experiment that will surely end his life, he figures he should be grateful Olson isn't around to see his demise.

Except, then Able is rescued. A group of shifters arrives and frees everyone, led by a grizzly shifter named Kontra Belikov. At first, Able fears that they killed his mate in the process, but Olson is nowhere to be found.

With the help of Kontra's gang, can Able figure out where Olson disappeared to?

Tracking the Guard
Copyright © 2021 Charlie Richards
ISBN: 978-1-4874-3341-3
Cover art by Angela Waters

Published by eXtasy Books Inc or
Devine Destinies, an imprint of eXtasy Books Inc

Look for us online at:
www.eXtasybooks.com or www.devinedestinies.com

Tracking the Guard
Kontra's Menagerie Book Thirty

By

Charlie Richards

DEDICATION

We must accept finite disappointment, but never lose infinite hope.
~Martin Luther King Jr.

CHAPTER ONE

So this is the end.

Able Lieder rested his head on his paws as he listened to the scientists plotting his demise. He'd known it would happen sooner or later. He'd been trapped in his leopard form for who knew how long, being poked and prodded by the assholes. This was the third place he remembered being at.

His one wish was that he could have seen his mate just one more time.

Except, Able hadn't seen the guard — who he knew only as Olson — in six days. The gorgeous black man had said goodbye to him that day, a sad smile curving his full lips when he'd discreetly tossed in a piece of beef jerky to him. Then Olson had left with a bowed head and the scent of sadness lingering in the air.

Olson had been one of the guards in Able's wing since the day he'd arrived. Able knew that the human didn't understand their connection. That didn't stop Olson from bringing Able treats and talking quietly to him, calling him a gorgeous cat, and even apologizing for what the scientists were doing to him.

It's probably for the best that Olson never knew we were soul mates.

The guard's loyalties would have ended up divided.

Able wouldn't have wished that fate on anyone and especially not his mate.

The thud of something heavy slamming into something else caught Able's attention. That was followed by shouts of

1

surprise from the scientists in the next room—the prep room, they called it. He'd never seen if he'd been taken beyond that place, as the tranquilizer they always used to sedate him so they could move him, knocked him out fully by the time they rolled him into the room on their trolley cart.

Able made out the unmistakable sound of flesh hitting flesh, then a body slamming into the wall. Rising to his feet, he pressed close to the bars. He looked that way just in time to watch a bleeding, screaming scientist push through the swinging door.

The man dashed with a limping gate down the hallway, whimpering as he went. Before he'd reached the door at the other end of the hall, which required a pass-card and a code to open, a hyena slammed open the swinging door. With a series of yips that sounded full of joy, the hyena galloped down the hallway.

As the hyena passed, Able noticed the intelligence gleaming in the male's eyes. Between that and the scent, he realized he was a shifter. Able sat on his haunches and watched as one of the worst tormentors of his life had his throat ripped out.

A dark wash of pleasure flooded Able—vengeance.

Couldn't have happened to a nicer asshole.

As the hyena turned and began peering into the cage at the end of the hall, the swinging door opened again. A dirty-blond-haired human dressed in black and carrying a gun appeared.

Able growled in warning to the hyena, which drew the gunman's attention.

"Hey, Payson," the human called. "This one feral?"

To Able's surprise, the hyena shifted. He crossed to Able's cage, as was usual for shifters, completely comfortable with his nudity. The human kept his gaze—and his gun—focused on Able.

Squatting in front of the cage, the hyena—Payson—grinned at him. "Not sure, Ryan," he replied, his gray eyes holding a wealth of mischievousness. "If your human half is still in there, rub your head against the cage bars."

Unable to help himself, Able rolled his eyes, even in cat form.

Ryan snorted and lowered his weapon. "Uh, I think he still understands us just fine." After placing his sidearm into the holster, he stated, "If you're going to stay in human form, you want my shirt?"

Scoffing, Payson shook his head. "Naw. Sam wouldn't like your scent all over me."

"What's the count?" a barrel-chested man demanded from where he stood holding the door open.

"Got two in here," Ryan replied. "A leopard shifter here" — he pointed at Able, then toward the cage Payson had been sniffing — "and a panda bear back there."

"Holy shit," the huge man grumbled. "How the hell did they get a panda bear over here?"

Payson shook his head, resting his fists on his hips. "Don't know, boss, but he's sedated." He focused on Able. "This one's awake." Cocking his head, Payson asked, "Can you shift?"

Able shook his head as the big male crossed to his cage, allowing him to scent him — a bear shifter of some sort.

"I'm Kontra Belikov," the man told him, tapping his chest. "This facility has being cleared of all enemies, so if I let you out, you can't attack anyone. Are we clear?"

Oh, shit! All enemies? My guard! I need to tell them.

Except, try as Able might, he still couldn't shift. He mewled softly, praying they would let him out. If he was freed, he could search the building and maybe stop these people from killing Olson, too.

"We'll take that as acceptance," Kontra stated, turning to the keypad. "Payson, grab the key card from that jerk over there." He pointed at the downed scientist. "Ryan, head into the lab and grab the rolling trolley for the panda as well as a lab coat for Payson."

"Yes, Alpha," Ryan replied before hurrying to do as he'd been ordered.

Payson returned with the card, and Kontra used it to open Able's cage. As soon as the door was wide enough, Able burst free. He heard Kontra's order to stop, but he ignored it.

Instead, Able tucked his head and used his shoulder to shove open the swinging door. He peered around the room, spotting Ryan as well as two others in black garb. There were three dead scientists as well . . . but no guards.

Spotting a door to the left, Able rushed through it, ignoring the cry of surprise from Ryan as well as the, "Leopard, wait!" from a dark-haired shifter with a scar on his face.

Able spotted a door propped open with another body and bolted through it. Unfortunately, he didn't know the layout of the place. Plus, a lot of the doors were closed and locked.

When Able needed to double back, he found himself face to face with Payson and Kontra, and he skidded to a stop.

"If you're looking for the way out," Kontra stated, narrowing his eyes. "We can show you, but you're in the middle of a swamp, so I recommend not going anywhere until we can get you all loaded into the box truck we have."

Huffing a sigh, Able tried to figure out a way to get his meaning across. He shook his head at the bear and chuffed softly, sharing his frustration.

"Oh, kitty charades," Payson cackled, clapping his hands and bouncing on his toes. "We can do this." Then he rested his hands on his hips and stated, "One chuff for yes. Two for no."

Able figured he should appreciate the fact that the pair were willing to try, even if he thought the hyena was a little on the crazy side. He dipped his chin in a nod.

Payson grinned broadly. "Are you trying to find the way out?"

Shaking his head, Able chuffed twice.

"Are you looking for something else?" Kontra asked.

If Able could have grimaced in cat form, he would have.

At Able's hesitation, Payson piped up, "Are you looking for some*one* else?"

Able quickly chuffed once.

Kontra and Payson exchanged looks before refocusing on Able. "A family member?" Kontra mused.

Chuffing twice, Able shifted his weight, getting antsy.

"Your mate?" Payson guessed.

Focusing on the weird yet perceptive hyena shifter, Able nodded again as he chuffed once.

"Human or shifter?" Kontra demanded. Then he rolled his eyes and amended, "One for human. Two for a paranormal."

Able chuffed once again.

"And you believe they're here?" Kontra pressed.

Uncertain how to respond to that, Able shook his head a little, then nodded.

"Not sure, huh?" Payson replied astutely. "Were you captured at the same time?"

After Able chuffed twice, Kontra pressed, "Then why do you think he or she is here?"

Payson's eyes widened. "Oh, shit. Is it someone working here?"

Able nodded, chuffing once.

Grimacing, Payson focused on Kontra. "No wonder he was eager to get out of the cage and look. We told him we were taking everyone out."

"Oh, fucking hell," Kontra grumbled, twisting his goateed lips into a deep scowl. "Guard or scientist?" Even as he asked, he started them to the left.

After another single chuff from Able, Kontra told him, "I'm taking you to the security room. We can use the monitors to look for your mate." His voice tightened as he lifted his hand to his ear, which held an earpiece. "Report on guards."

With Able's shifter hearing, he was able to hear half a dozen men reporting off that all guards were down. He couldn't help it. He mewled as distress swamped him.

"Hey, relax, kitty," Payson urged, patting his shoulders twice. "Fate wouldn't give you a mate just to have him or her taken away again." He grinned widely even as he continued walking the hall nude. "Hell, she gave me a mate, so you know she loves shifters to get their happily ever after." With a wink, Payson added, "Even the crazy ones."

Able heaved a soft sigh.

Huh. At least, he knows he's crazy. Odd.

Kontra pulled out a tablet and activated it.

Able noticed a map on it and followed eagerly as the bear shifter began to jog.

Lifting his hand to his ear again, Kontra stated, "Lamar, I'm coming to you. I need you to pull up every camera that has a guard on it."

"Yes, Alpha," a melodious tenor replied. After a second, he asked, "May I ask why?"

"Because one of the rescued shifters thinks one of the guards is his mate," Kontra replied bluntly.

"Ah, crap," Lamar replied.

That was followed by several other men cursing.

Evidently, it was an open line.

"God damn it," a deep voice grumbled. "Did we just take out a shifter's mate?"

"I sure as hell hope not," Kontra replied. "But if we did, then it was part of Fate's plan because she's got a better mate lined up for him."

"Male or female," Lamar asked. "So I can narrow down the pictures."

Kontra peered down at Able and arched one brow.

Able chuffed once, indicating the former.

"Male," Kontra repeated.

"Okay."

Able felt a measure of surprise that no one said anything about that.

Evidently, Payson picked up on it through his scent. He snickered before saying, "We're all gay or bi here, kitty." His grin widened as he added, "You and your mate will be in good company with us."

"Once the guard answers for his crimes against our kind," Kontra commented.

Unable to help himself, Able growled.

Scoffing, Payson didn't sound impressed when he replied, "Relax, kitty. He'll survive it."

Able rumbled with annoyance.

He better.

They reached the control room without further comment. When they entered, a twink-like blond spun his chair to face them. A huge, armed redhead—a human—in their same black outfit appeared to be guarding him.

"Here's the first set, Alpha," Lamar claimed, pointing at the bank of nine screens. His expression appeared kind as he focused on Able. "Let me know when you need me to flip to the next screen."

Able heaved his front paws onto the counter and peered closer at the screens. After a quick sweep, he didn't recognize any of the men. He chuffed once with a glance at Lamar.

Lamar punched a couple of buttons, and the pictures changed.

Once again, Able didn't see Olson on the screen.

Each time Lamar changed the screens and Able didn't spot his mate, his pulse sped up a little as hope filled him.

"These are the last ones," Lamar told him softly, changing the screens once more.

After another review, Able eased back to sit on his haunches. He shook his head. Concern and elation filled him in equal measure.

Payson squeezed his shoulder. "Well, damn. That's good news, eh?" Grinning widely, he added, "He ain't here."

Able nodded once.

So where is he?

As if Lamar had heard his thoughts, he began tapping the computer again. "Well, there are probably guards in these guys' employ that aren't here." He hummed before continuing, "Let's see who's on the list."

"You know what would be good news," the big redhead grumbled, crossing his arms over his chest as he scowled. "Is if you put on some fucking pants."

Payson tipped his head back and cackled.

CHAPTER TWO

Running the sander over the wood of his deck, Olson Caynar allowed his mind to drift. As it did each time he didn't stay focused, his thoughts turned to the job he'd quit. Olson wondered what happened to the leopard he'd found utterly fascinating and gorgeous.

It's probably dead now.

Olson winced. Even though the scientists claimed they never injured any of the animals—that the ones that had disappeared had been transferred to other locations—he didn't actually believe that. Olson had spotted at least two corpses being removed by the elite guards—the ones that lived on-site.

I'm glad I'm not one of those. They were all belligerent assholes.

Shaking his head, Olson refocused on his work. He knew he would need to find a new job before too long, but he was taking a couple of weeks to decide what he wanted to do with his life. Olson was also doing a number of odd jobs that had been piling up because of all the hours the scientists had insisted on.

That's such an odd place.

Olson had been tempted to poke his nose into the place and seek out their secrets. Then he'd seen the first dead animal—a large lynx. Recalling the old adage that curiosity killed the cat, he decided it would be better to keep his nose out of it.

Then that leopard had arrived.

Knowing he wouldn't be able to continue watching the scientists run experiments on the magnificent animal, he'd had to walk away. He'd been tempted to report them to environmentalists and was still debating the idea. He didn't have any proof of abuse, but he didn't think he would need it to at least get an investigation started.

Shaking his head, Olson focused on his work. He needed to finish it that afternoon so he could move on to staining it before the weather changed. Olson knew rain in the bayou could happen at any time.

After another hour, Olson turned off the sander and sat back on his haunches. He admired his work, sliding his palm over the boards. Grunting in appreciation, he nodded and rose to his feet.

Olson rounded his old Victorian home, heading to a detached garage. After putting the sander away, he picked up the cans of stain. He was carrying them toward the back of his home when he heard the sound of an engine.

Scowling, Olson put down the cans as he watched a large black quad-cab truck appear between the large cypress trees that surrounded his secluded home. He didn't recognize the vehicle, and he didn't have any friends that would splurge for something like that. Hell, Olson barely had any friends—period.

They'd all deserted him when his wife had divorced him.
No big loss, though.

When the driver's side door opened and a man stepped out, Olson realized he recognized him—Chase. The guy had been one of the on-site, elite guards at the clinic. He had no idea how the man knew where he lived or even why he would visit him.

Guess I'll find out.

Leaving his cans of stain behind, Olson headed toward the man. He saw him remove his sunglasses as he peered around the area. Chase's sneer as he took in Olson's slightly dilapidated home was unmistakable.

Yep. Still an asshole.

"Figures you'd live in a dump like this," Chase commented rudely. Glaring, he crossed his arms over his chest. "How much did they pay you? Huh, Olson?"

"Pay me?" Olson frowned at the impolite ex-coworker. "What the hell are you talking about? What are you even doing here?"

"I'm here to find out how they contacted you." Chase placed his sunglasses on the hood of his truck before cracking his knuckles. "Then I'm gonna kick the shit out of you for picking paranormals over your own kind before taking you in."

With each word Chase spoke, Olson became more and more confused. The man had to be delusional or on something. One thing stood out, though—he intended to attack him.

Olson shifted his left foot back a little, preparing to defend himself. Having been in the military for nearly two decades before going into the private sector, he had plenty of training. Except, he'd seen the elite guards at the company move with the grace and speed of a ninja while handling some of the larger animals.

Taking out Chase wouldn't be easy. That meant negotiating and explanations were the better options.

"I have no idea what you're talking about," Olson repeated his denial. "No one contacted me about paying for anything." Unable to completely contain his curiosity, Olson added, "Who would contact me about what?"

"The men who are paying for the repairs on this dump." Chase once again cast his gaze over Olson's old Victorian. "That's the only way you could afford to quit working. They needed information on how to get past security, and you gave it to them," he declared, pointing a finger at Olson's chest. "You betrayed your own kind."

Olson watched Chase's face take on a pinkish hue, betraying his rage just as much as his raising voice did. "Someone got past security?" He struggled to comprehend what Chase was telling him. "Who would bother to do that?"

"The shifters, you dolt," Chase claimed, staring at him as if he were an idiot. "You betrayed humankind for shifters!"

Before Olson could even guess at what the hell Chase was talking about, the man lunged and swung. The guy was so angry that he gave away his intent by turning his hips. That gave Olson just enough time to pivot and block.

"Knock this shit off and listen to me," Olson demanded, wondering if Chase would believe anything he said. "I don't know what shifters are. No one paid me anything. And I quit because I didn't like the hours."

Most of that was true, anyway.

"I can tell you're lying," Chase stated, curling his lip. "Who contacted you?" He shifted his feet, obviously readying to attack again. "Make this easy on yourself and tell me."

"Tell me what the fuck happened," Olson ordered instead, doing his best to figure out Chase's next move. "Did something happen at the facility?"

Did someone beat him to telling environmentalists?

What happened to the cat?

"As if you don't know," Chase countered. "I come back from vacation to a destroyed building. I bet they killed everyone there, and you're gonna pay for it."

Shocked by Chase's declaration, Olson didn't react fast enough. The man's fist slammed into his jaw, causing him to stumble back. His momentum bounced him into Chase's truck. When the back of his head rapped against the window, Olson grunted.

Olson barely spotted it when Chase followed up with a jab to his gut, and he doubled over as pain spiked through his stomach. The elbow to his spine sent Olson crashing to the ground. He rolled instinctively, just knowing a kick would be coming next.

Chase still managed to clip his hip.

"Son of a bitch, you moron," Olson roared, finally finding his tongue again. He continued to roll right onto his knees. "You're out of your fucking mind!"

Seeing another kick coming, Olson caught Chase's leg and tucked it close to his body. He pushed on the man's knee, sending him sprawling to his back. Taking advantage, Olson leaped to his feet and ran toward his house.

Olson heard Chase roar his name and knew he only had seconds to make a decision.

How do I get away from this crazy man?

As Olson dashed through his front door and into his foyer, he spotted his keys in the candy dish. While grabbing them, he slammed the door shut. Just in time, too, because a loud thump shuddered against it.

After quickly locking it, Olson ran down the hall toward the back. As he reached the back door, he heard glass shatter. He grimaced, knowing if he got away from the asshole, he would have another project to fix.

"Damn it all," Olson grumbled under his breath.

Olson grabbed his porch railing and leaped over it. His head spun a little, reminding him that he'd already had it slammed against glass. His chest and torso twinged, too.

Doing his best to ignore it, Olson raced back to the garage, relieved that he'd left the main doors open. He bypassed his *Jeep* and jumped on his dirt bike. With a quick crank of the key, it fired to life, and he gunned it.

To Olson's surprise, Chase was already over halfway across his yard. He couldn't believe how fast the man could move. Tearing out of the yard, he headed toward town, having every intention of reporting Chase's attack.

When Olson heard Chase's truck fire to life, he hit the throttle, urging his small dirt bike to go faster. His tires spun over the rutted dirt of the back road. He wobbled a little before getting his bike back on track.

Hitting a better stretch of the road, Olson took a chance and glanced behind him. He spotted Chase through the windshield of his truck. His eyes seemed to blaze with his anger.

"What the hell is wrong with this guy?" Olson muttered under his breath, recognizing Chase's intent.

He knew the guy was going to try to run him off the road. On a dirt bike, he could potentially drive into the cypress forest, but he knew the ground was so marshy, he could wreck very easily. His brain whirled with options.

"You brought this on yourself," Chase screamed, shouting out his window. "I'm gonna catch you, Olson. I'm gonna take you in, and we're gonna torture the fuck out of you for what you did."

Olson gritted his teeth and navigated around another pothole, then a deep rut. While he would have had a better chance of getting away in his *Jeep*, he knew he wouldn't have been able to get past the truck parked in his driveway. Olson figured that had been Chase's plan . . . and now he was paying for it.

Just as Olson feared he would need to brave the trees, he heard the roar of more engines — powerful motorcycle ones.

What the hell?

Having one guest on his road was rare, but having multiple ones?

Olson spotted a couple of *Harleys*, and he couldn't imagine driving such a high-end motorcycle on the crappy back road. Still, he didn't have time to stop and marvel. To Olson's relief, the men on the motorcycles pulled to opposite sides of the road, clearing a way.

Taking a chance, as Olson raced by the men, he hollered, "Call the cops. This asshole's trying to kill me."

Then Olson was past them, and he prayed at least one of them would have a cell phone with service so far deep in the bayou. When their engines immediately rumbled to life, Olson figured he hadn't gotten his wish. A glance behind him offered a surprise — the men on the *Harleys* were following the truck.

Damn. Are they with Chase?

A second later, Olson's question was answered when the only man not on a *Harley* — instead, he drove a bullet bike at excessive speeds on a dangerous road — zipped to the driver's side window. He cackled a little as he punched through the open window, landing the strike on Chase.

Chase lost control of his truck, crashing head-on into a huge cypress tree.

In the next instant, that same man pulled even with Olson. He flipped up his visor and grinned at him. "Hey, Olson. We've been lookin' for you."

Upon hearing his name from the stranger's lips, shock flooded Olson. He missed noticing a rut, and his front tire slipped. With a cry of alarm, he went down.

For the second time in such a short while, Olson slammed his head into something — this time the ground. Black spots swam across his vision, and his entire body throbbed.

"Damn it, Payson," a deep voice rumbled. "You weren't supposed to shock him into losing control."

"Sorry, boss," the stranger — Payson — replied. "I only meant to —"

Olson didn't hear more as unconsciousness took him.

CHAPTER THREE

Growling softly, Able felt his frustration mounting. It had been three days since he'd been freed, and he still couldn't shift. That meant he couldn't leave their secluded campsite in the woods to search for his mate.

Instead, Able had to wait for Kontra's people to do things for him. It didn't help that communication was still a guessing game. He was so very tired of one chuff for yes and two chuffs for no.

"Hey, kitty," a tenor voice called. "You around?"

Able did his best to roll his eyes while in cat form. Since Payson had started calling him that, all the gang was calling him that. Still, Able wouldn't ignore the speaker. He could have some important news, after all.

Rumbling softly, Able half-rose and leaned a little over the edge of the tree branch where he'd been lying. He spotted Yuma, a penguin shifter. All the gang had been kind, telling him their names and animals. Able found learning all that was a bit overwhelming. They were a really big gang.

Yuma peered up at him, probably drawn by the noise. "Hey, kitty." He grinned widely. "I just got a call from Kontra. They found Olson."

Able straightened, tipping his head to the side and rumbling inquisitively.

Meeting his gaze, Yuma rubbed the back of his neck. "The thing is" — his smile dimmed — "he was being chased by someone in a pick-up truck." He furrowed his brows. "Payson made that guy crash. Then Olson sort of lost control of the dirt bike he was fleeing on." Resting his hands on his hips, Yuma finished, "So, Eli checked him out and found a few bruises and stuff. They're gonna bring him here as soon as—"

Growling, Able had heard enough. He dropped from the tree and bumped Yuma's hip lightly.

Yuma touched Able's head gently. "Don't worry," he assured. "My guys are really good at handling these sorts of problems. They'll get him taken care of."

Able bobbed his head in a slight nod, then began padding back to the main camp. The group had pretty much rented the entire campground, with only a few outsiders near the entrance. That allowed shifting, as long as they were discreet and careful.

Reaching the edge of a campsite, Able sat, idly flicking his tale. He stared in the direction he knew the motorcycles had to come.

Yuma stood next to him. "I don't know how long they'll be."

Able flicked an ear in acknowledgment of Yuma's comment, but he didn't move other than that.

Hunter, Yuma's human mate, approached. "Told him we found his mate, huh?" As Yuma nodded, Hunter placed the camp chair he'd been holding on the ground. "Well, let's get comfortable then."

After settling in the chair, Hunter helped Yuma sit on his lap. "So, I'm not going to ask you questions," Yuma's mate stated, glancing his way with a smile. "I figure you're tired of struggling to communicate enough as it is."

Rumbling softly, Able appreciated Hunter's comment.

"Instead, I'm going to wonder if Olson knows about shifters." Scoffing softly, Hunter added, "And if he doesn't, boy is he about to be in for a rude awakening."

"Think about it, though," Adam stated, closing the distance with his own chair. "I overheard you on the phone with Kontra, Yuma." He placed his chair on Able's other side before relaxing in it. "If Olson has someone after him, then he could use our brand of help."

Hunter snorted as Yuma snickered.

Able wasn't certain what that meant, but considering they'd freed him from asshole scientists, he had to trust them.

A number of the other guys joined them as Able sat in silence, waiting. The men chatted amongst themselves, talking motorcycles, changes on the Shifter Council, and sex. It seemed the group enjoyed trying to embarrass each other.

Considering Able hadn't had sex in almost a year and a half, he looked forward to getting to put an end to his dry spell.

Of course, that would take shifting first, damn it.

Just as that thought flittered through his mind, Able made out the roar of motorcycle engines. He straightened a bit more, flicking his ears in anticipation. His heart pounded, and his whiskers twitched.

"Relax, kitty," Adam rumbled, petting down his spine lightly. "If he doesn't know you're a shifter, we don't want to freak him out."

Able glanced Adam's way, then returned his focus to the approaching group. Spotting Kontra in the lead, he swept his gaze over the motorcycles following him. He noticed Sam—a small wolf shifter who was mated with Eli, the gang's pack doctor—driving a small, street-legal dirt bike. When he searched out Eli, he saw a familiar figure sitting behind the python shifter.

Olson. Olson Caynar. My mate.

Able had learned not only Olson's last name from the employee files that Lamar had pulled, but also that he'd quit. While he wasn't certain how he felt about his mate walking away from him, Able tried to be understanding about it. After all, Olson had no idea that they were mates . . . if he even knew about shifters and mates at all.

"We're here," Kontra stated needlessly. "Let's get you comfortable. There's someone here who really wants to see you."

After dismounting from behind Eli, and pausing a second to steady himself on the back of the python shifter's motorcycle, Olson turned toward Kontra and stated, "Payson said you'd been looking for me, but no one has told me why."

Kontra's goateed lips lifted into a slight smile. "I didn't think you'd believe me unless I actually showed you." Smirking, he beckoned him forward, while turning toward where the gang had clustered together to sit. "No fainting now. Can't have you hitting your head again."

Olson scoffed. "Nice vote of confidence." He glanced around at all the men, appearing just a little nervous. "Look. I appreciate the assist and all, but what the hell is going on?" Then Olson's gaze riveted on Able. "Holy shit," he whispered. "That's the cat. The leopard." Olson's eyes widened, and he froze. "You're the ones Chase was talking about. You destroyed the facility."

Kontra continued to stroll toward Able slowly, drawing Olson with him. "We did destroy the facility you used to work at," the grizzly shifter confirmed. "They were doing experiments on our kind. We don't take too kindly to that."

"Our kind?" Olson repeated, sounding oh-so-confused. "God, Chase was talking odd shit, too." He glanced around the group. "What the hell is going on, and why were you looking for me?"

Well, that answers that . . . he doesn't know about shifters.

For some reason, Able felt a wave of relief upon finding that out.

"Well, we have a bit of a tale to share with you, Olson," Kontra told him. He paused about ten feet from the group of men and glanced around. "Who's cooking dinner?"

Yuma eased from Hunter's lap. "I'll cook, but someone else has to tend the fire."

"On it," Hunter immediately stated, also rising.

Kontra indicated the vacated chair. "Have a seat, Olson."

Olson looked at Kontra with an expression that clearly betrayed that he thought the big man had a few screws loose. After all, the chair was right beside where Able was sitting . . . in leopard form.

Payson patted Olson's shoulder. "It's okay, man. He won't hurt ya." Then he waggled his eyebrows. "Except maybe in the best way possible . . . once he shifts."

"Shifts." Olson glanced around at everyone again, scowling, before murmuring, "Chase used that word, too. Shifters." Rubbing the back of his neck, Olson muttered, "What the hell does that mean?"

Adam reached over and rubbed Able's fur again. "You wanna try one more time, kitty?"

Able growled in annoyance, since he couldn't very well tell them that he'd been trying almost non-stop for the last three days. Still, he took in a deep breath and prepared to try once more. His nostrils were flooded with Olson's magnificent scent, and he nearly moaned with the pleasure of it.

Finally, Able felt the shift begin. Agony tore through his body as his muscles popped, his bones cracked, and his tendons rearranged. He let out a low yowl of pain, his back arching, when his tail retracted and his head reshaped.

Spots danced across Able's vision as he flopped to his ass and panted harshly. He felt a hand on his upper arm, lending support, and he realized without Adam's grip, he probably would have toppled over completely. Unable to help himself, Able leaned into the white tiger shifter's strength as he caught his breath.

"That sounded painful," Adam commented softly. "You could have waited another day. Someone else could have shown him."

Able blinked to clear his vision and lifted his head. "No," he croaked, his voice rough from disuse and his cry. "It needed to be me."

Then Able focused on Olson, taking in his shocked expression. He would bet that if Olson hadn't had gorgeous medium-brown skin, he would have been as pale as a ghost. His mate even took a step back when their eyes met, causing Able's gut to clench a bit.

"My name is Able Lieder, Olson," he told him softly. "I'm a leopard shifter."

"O-Okay." Then Olson's eyes rolled to the back of his head, and he began to fall.

As much as Able wished he could have caught Olson himself, he knew he didn't have the strength. He was still a little uncoordinated himself.

Fortunately, Kontra seemed to have been ready. He swung Olson into his arms and stared at Able. "I'm going to lay him down in a tent. Why don't you get some food, then join him?" Sweeping his gaze over him, Kontra added, "You're thin. How long did they hold you for?"

"Not sure," Able admitted before swallowing to get a bit of moisture into his too-dry throat. "What day is it?"

Adam handed Able his beer, and he took a couple of grateful gulps. Even as he winced at the flavor, as he wasn't a big fan of beer, he appreciated the moisture to his throat. Upon hearing the date, Able nearly choked on his mouthful.

Once Able had managed to swallow it, he mumbled, "Fucking hell. Longer than I thought." Handing back Adam's beer, he shook his head. "I must have been unconscious a lot." Able met Kontra's gaze. "Almost six months. They snagged me while I was out running alone."

"You were reported missing by your pride, but no clues as

to your whereabouts had been found," Lamar told him, staring at his tablet screen. Peering his way, he held up his device and explained, "A list from the Shifter Council. They're the ones that ordered us to clear that facility."

Rubbing his palms over his face, Able sighed. "Thank you for that." He met Kontra's gaze. "They were going to kill me the next day."

"I'm glad we arrived in time," Kontra replied.

"Me, too," Able murmured.

Kontra turned and began carrying Olson away, and Able barely managed to hold back his growl, as irrational as it was.

"Come on, kitty," Adam urged, helping Able to his feet. "Let's get you and your mate a big meal and head to the tent. You should definitely be there when he wakes." With a smirk, he added, "Maybe you can explain while sharing the food."

"M'name's Able," he corrected because he was getting damn tired of hearing people call him kitty.

Damn that crazy Payson.

"Sure, kitty," Adam replied with a grin and a wink.

"Ugh. That name's gonna stick, isn't it?"

Payson chuckled. "Yup."

CHAPTER FOUR

The dull edges of pain roused Olson. Remaining still, he cataloged his aches before pressing his memory for how he'd received them. Olson stiffened as he recalled everything that had recently happened—his crazed ex-coworker, the help from biker strangers, and seeing the cat do . . . *that.*

That really happened, right?

"Yes, Olson," a soft rumbling voice murmured. "That really happened."

"Didn't realize I'd said that out loud," Olson mumbled.

Or that I wasn't alone.

Olson cracked open his eyelids and spotted some type of canvas overhead. *I'm in a tent. Right. The bikers took me to a campground.* Hearing the rustle of blankets, Olson turned his head . . . and sucked in a surprised breath.

"You're him," Olson whispered, tensing. Except, that caused his aches to intensify, so he forced himself to relax again. "You were the cat." Realizing what he said, he added, "But how is that possible?"

"We're here," he murmured. "All around you. We always have been." His smile seemed to soften his hard features as he stared intently at him. "Hiding in plain sight. We've never meant you any harm."

The hazel-eyed man set the plate on his lap aside and leaned toward him, causing his short, strawberry-blond hair to fall over his forehead. Reaching toward him, he touched Olson's shoulder gently, almost reverently. Then he skimmed his fingertips down his arm until he took his hand in his own.

23

Olson had enjoyed the intimacy of a man a few times, but never had he felt a surge of arousal just from the touch of a man's hand. He swallowed hard as his blood heated in his veins. The tingles that caused goose bumps to erupt on his arm overrode his instinct to pull away.

"Wh-Who are you?" Olson mumbled.

"Able," the man immediately replied. "Able Lieder." Lifting their combined hands, he pecked a kiss to Olson's knuckle. "How long did you work for those assholes before quitting?" He eyed him carefully as he continued, "Why did you work for them? Why did you quit? Why were you being chased by that other guard?"

"Whoa, whoa." Olson squeezed the hand he held. "One question at a time." That was when he noticed something else. "Are you naked?"

That idea caused Olson's prick to thicken the rest of the way, arousal swimming through his veins. He couldn't help but admire the broad-shouldered man's wide pectorals, which tapered to a trim waist—a waist that seemed a little lean. Olson could make out the treasure trail that disappeared beneath the blanket Able had over his lap.

Olson sniffed the air, twice, before a lascivious smile curved his lips. "Yes." He used his free hand to tease the edge of the blanket down his thigh, revealing a bit more hints of his groin . . . and how it appeared that the fabric became caught on something thick.

"Shit," Olson mumbled, even as his breathing hitched. "Stop." He shook his head. "We shouldn't be thinking with our dicks. We should be talking and explaining." Still, Olson couldn't tear his gaze away from where Able slipped the blanket over a bit more, giving Olson a teasing glimpse of hard flesh. When he spoke again, he would forever deny how breathy he sounded, "Y-You asked qu-questions, and I know I have some of my own."

Freezing, Able twisted his full lips into a grimace.

And damn, when do I look at men's lips?

Olson had never kissed a guy in his life. To his relief—mixed with disappointment—he watched Able pull the blanket a bit higher again. Then Able squeezed his hand and brought it to his lips once more.

"My apologies, my mate," Able crooned roughly. "After scenting you for so long and having no hope of doing anything about it." His expression turned strained. "Then not seeing you for several days, only to think you'd died in the attack." Able stared at him with what could only be called a hungry look. "Now you're here, with me, after being attacked by someone you'd been working with. And I can scent your arousal, and it is delicious." He shook his head. "I'm having trouble focusing."

Olson only understood about half of what Able had just rambled, but he got the gist that the guy was in the same state of confused arousal as himself. Spotting the plate of food Able had set aside, he pointed at it. At the same time, his stomach rumbled.

"How about we get more of that." Olson thought the brat in a bun looked and smelled damn delicious. *Plus, potato salad and chips. Yum!* "We'll ask our questions of each other, and maybe come to some understanding of what the hell is going on."

Able nodded and, after a second of hesitation, released Olson's hand.

Olson was surprised at how much he missed the contact.

Reaching behind him, Able picked up something. He turned back around and revealed two more plates of food. One contained four more brat-dogs. The second held a large helping of potato salad as well as fruit salad and red *Jello*. Once Able had placed the food between them, he grabbed an unopened bag of barbeque-flavored potato chips.

Easing to a sitting position, Olson stared at all the offerings, and his mouth watered. "Planning ahead?" he guessed.

Shrugging one shoulder, Able admitted, "The guys here have some experience with explaining shifters to humans. It was their idea."

Nodding, Olson murmured, "Shifters and humans." They were back to that again. After accepting a fork from Able, he asked, "Soooo, you can really turn into a cat? A leopard?"

Able nodded as he stabbed his fork into a slice of banana. "I do. That's why the scientists captured me." He held Olson's gaze as he told him, "According to Kontra, there have been human organizations who've captured and experimented on us for decades. He's helped shut down a great number of their installations, but more just seem to keep popping up again."

"Why do they want to experiment on you?" Olson asked before eating his bite of potato salad. He hummed appreciatively at the flavor bursting across his tongue. Whoever had made it had used the perfect amount of dill.

"Kontra said there were various reasons, but the most prevalent is to find easy ways to kill us and to figure out how to splice our genes into humans to enhance their strength, speed, and stuff."

Recalling the way the top guards at the facility moved, Olson whispered, "That's what they did to Chase and the other guys."

"Who's Chase?"

Upon hearing the growl in Able's voice, Olson snapped his focus back to the man's face. *When had he started ogling his chest again?* If Olson had to guess at the expression on Able's face, he would call it . . . jealousy.

Huh.

"Chase is the guard that attacked me at my home today," Olson answered. "The guys stopped him. I don't know what happened to him."

Able's countenance immediately eased.

Yep, it'd been jealousy.

"Enhanced humans would explain how they could capture me while I was out running," Able seemed to muse. "I never heard or saw them coming until I'd been hit with a tranquilizer dart. Then I woke in a cage and couldn't shift to ask who they were or what the hell they wanted."

"So Kontra's people were able to answer that for you," Olson guessed. When Able nodded, something else flitted through Olson's brain. "Could you, uh . . . well" — he struggled with how to phrase it — "when you're a cat, you could still, um, did you know what was going on around you?"

Able nodded. "Yes. When shifters are in their animal form, they're completely cognizant. They can think and reason as a human," he continued to explain. "It's just a different form with a simpler set of instincts."

"Well, damn." Olson tried to wrap his mind around that. "No wonder so many of the animals at the facility" — he glanced at Able — "uh, shifters there looked so frustrated and angry."

Able simply nodded as he took a bite of his brat-dog.

Before following Able's example and taking a big bite of his own brat-dog, Olson asked, "How come you never growled at me?" He recalled those days, saying, "I mean, you always watched me like a hawk, but you were never aggressive the way other animals were."

For a second, Able froze. Then he swallowed what was in his mouth and cleared his throat. "You're my mate, Olson," he told him, using that term once more.

Olson ate his own bite of dog before admitting, "I don't know what that means, Able."

Setting down his half-eaten dog, Able licked his lips. He looked a mixture of excitement, anticipation, and trepidation as he stared at Olson.

"To a shifter, finding their mate is one of the greatest things to ever happen to them," Able began slowly. "We can wait centuries to be gifted by Fate with our mate . . . the other half of our soul. The person who will complete us."

A mixture of shock and disbelief filled Olson. He took a bite of his brat-dog, buying himself a few seconds to think. His brain whirled with the implications of those words.

Mate. Fate. Other half of our soul.

Once Olson had swallowed, he grabbed a napkin and wiped his fingers. He held Able's gaze as he began repeating what he thought he understood. "So, people who can turn into an animal exist. They're called shifters. And those ass-holes at the facility where I worked knowingly experimented on them, even though they know they're sentient." When Able didn't say anything, Olson continued, "And shifters believe in Fate-given soul mates." After another second of hesitation, Olson added, "And you believe I'm that person to you?" Still nothing. "Why?"

Able finally smiled. "Yes, to everything you said, and the reason why is simple enough." Reaching out, he once again took Olson's hand. "Shifters recognize their mate by their scent. Even over the acrid and nasty smells in that lab, your scent cut through it all. Every time you were near, your masculine smell filled my senses and flooded me with need." To Olson's surprise, Able's cheeks pinked a little before he stated, "It was so damn difficult to keep from springing a boner in cat form. Never had that trouble before."

That sounded more than a little odd to Olson, so he chose to ignore it. Instead, he shook his head and asked, "So, you don't choose your mate. You believe Fate does it for you?" As Able opened his mouth while nodding, Olson quickly added, "So, you wouldn't care one wit about me if I weren't your mate?"

Furrowing his brows, Able countered, "Why did you quit?"

Confused by the subject change, Olson opened his mouth, then closed it again. Embarrassment filled him as he realized the truth. "I couldn't watch them keep you in a cage." He frowned. "How they were treating you was wrong."

"Your file said you'd been working there for several months before I was transferred to them." Able didn't sound accusatory. He was just stating a fact. "You didn't seem to have a problem with how they treated the animals then."

Olson shook his head. "Not true. I didn't like it on the others, either."

Able squeezed Olson's hand. "But seeing them do it to me was the push you needed to walk away." His expression turned understanding. "That's what Fate does. When mates come together, even if the circumstances aren't ideal, she gives the pair that push they need to make changes, allowing them to be together." With a heated look, Able swept his gaze over Olson's body. "If we'd walked past each other on the sidewalk, we would have been attracted to each other, anyway."

Thinking he understood, he murmured, "So, Fate just helps us overcome our inhibitions."

"Exactly."

Olson blew out a breath as he eyed the handsome man sitting next to him. "So, uh, what exactly does that mean for us?"

The feral light that gleamed in Able's eyes caused Olson's heartrate to spike. He suddenly felt as if he were prey. When it came to coupling, that was a first for him.

"Well, I'm going to fuck you," Able told him bluntly. Lifting his free hand, he once again touched the point where Olson's neck met his shoulder. "And I'm going to bite you right here, claiming you and bonding our life lines." Then Able pinned him with an earnest expression. "After that, we'll figure out a way to create a life together, and since I'm only a little over a hundred years old, that'll be several centuries."

Olson gaped. "What?"

CHAPTER FIVE

Able winced. "Right. I still have a few things to explain," he whispered. At least Olson wasn't trying to pull away.

"How old are you?"

Oh, that's what he got stuck on.

"I'm one hundred and two," Able admitted.

"Damn, shifters age well," Olson mumbled, sweeping his gaze over him. "You don't look a day over thirty-five."

Smiling slightly, Able explained, "Well, shifters live upward of five hundred, so once we reach our prime, our aging pretty much comes to a standstill." Squeezing the hand he still held, "You'll stop aging, too."

Olson gazed at him in shock. "I hope the scientists never figure out that bonding with a shifter is like the fountain of youth."

Able chuckled as he shook his head. "It only works if the pair is matched by Fate." Grimacing, he added, "But, yeah, it's one of the reasons shifters don't randomly tell humans about them. It's already dangerous enough."

When Olson did nothing but stare and nod, Able racked his brain for some way to move forward. His engorged cock still throbbed, and he desperately wanted to sink it into his mate. He'd been around him for so long and never been able to do anything. Sitting naked beside him was a test of Able's control that he feared he might lose.

"I want to lay you down, Olson," Able blurted, admiring Olson's smooth, dark skin. "Sink into you and revel in your hard, sexy body."

"You want to bond us," Olson whispered.

Even though it wasn't a question, Able answered anyway. "With every fiber of my being." Upon seeing the way Olson's lips quirked at his choice words, he fought back a blush. Still, Able admitted, "When my new friends found you, you were injured and fleeing for your life. My instincts are screaming to bond us, to keep you safe and gift you with the blessings that come with mating a shifter."

"Wh-What blessings?" Even as Olson asked, his deep brown eyes darkened nearly to black. The heady scent of his arousal thickened, flooding the small tent. He cleared his throat and added, "And maybe we should talk about that, too, first. My ex-coworker." Olson frowned. "I don't know what happened to him. Do you? He could still be a danger to you if you're around me." Shaking his head, he added, "He said he was taking me in. I don't know where. I would never forgive myself if you were captured again, too."

Able wanted to yowl with pleasure that Olson seemed not only receptive, but also that he cared enough already to worry about him.

Controlling himself, Able explained, "Not only will your life extend to match mine, but your body will become stronger. You'll be able to move faster and heal more quickly."

Scoffing, the sound one of amusement, Olson smiled. "So, not only the fountain of youth, but your fated mates also get the benefits without going through genetic engineering."

Snorting, Able nodded. "Guess so." Addressing his comment about his safety, he pointed out, "It doesn't seem you're so safe, at the moment, either. I'd like it if we stay with these guys for a while until whoever Chase is working for is caught."

Even as Olson scowled, he nodded. "Yeah, I can see the wisdom in that." He peered off to the right, silent thoughts flitting across his face. "He knows where I live, so others must, too."

Able brought Olson's hand to his lips. Turning their wrists, he pressed a kiss to his palm. The move brought his mate's attention back to him, just as he'd hoped.

"You're very receptive to this," Able whispered against Olson's flesh. "Do you mind telling me why?"

As Able waited for Olson to answer, he began moving their half-eaten plates out of the way. Call him an optimist, but if his human gave him even the slightest indication, Able would be on him so fast. He didn't want to make a mess out of the blankets.

I also don't want to seem unappreciative of the gang's gift.

They'd bought tents for every shifter they'd rescued, which happened to be six, including himself.

"I was in the military for almost two decades," Olson revealed, his nostrils flaring as he stared at where Able nuzzled and kissed his palm. "Things happen in back alleys that are damn tough to explain." Sweeping his gaze over Able's bare torso, Olson stated, "Knowing there are shifters out there, maybe other paranormals" — since he phrased it as a question, Able nodded his head in confirmation, urging his mate to continue—"well, it explains a few things. Are vampires real, too?"

Able chuckled softly. "They are." With the dishes all out of the way, he leaned toward Olson, using his own body to push him back onto the blankets. "But I'll explain them later."

When Able dipped his head, angling for Olson's mouth, his human tensed. "What are you doing?"

Even though Able thought his movements were pretty self-explanatory, he still answered. "I'm going to kiss you, Olson." He saw the way his soon-to-be lover's brows furrowed. "I wish to taste you, to tease your tongue with my own."

Olson cleared his throat, the scent of discomfort beating out the arousal. "Never kissed a guy before."

Able paused, resting his hand on Olson's chest. Gently teasing his palm over his pectoral, he adjusted their twined fingers so he could lightly massage his palm. Taking in Olson's tension, Able realized he might need to slow his roll.

Damn.

"Have you done *anything* with a guy?" Able asked softly. While he had no desire to discuss his mate's past interactions, he needed to get a gist of his experience.

Olson cleared his throat as his brows furrowed a little. "Fucked a few while overseas," he told him gruffly. "After my wife divorced me, I became a little less . . . discerning. If I had an itch and he was willing to scratch it—" Olson shrugged one shoulder, not needing to finish.

Able understood.

"But you've never kissed one and have never been on the receiving end."

Watching his mate shake his head, Able felt a surge of possessiveness. "Then *I* am the only one who will ever get to enjoy those things with you."

Able gripped the blanket and adjusted it, allowing him to slide his bare leg over Olson's jeans-clad one. Easing his hips close, he moved his hand up so he could tease at his nipple. All the while, Able kept his weight on his right elbow and forearm while using the fingers of that hand to massage Olson's palm.

"Relax," Able crooned, lowering his head. Seeing Olson's continued tension, he didn't angle for his mouth right away. "Everything between mates is amplified," he whispered into his human's ear as he nuzzled the crook of his neck. Licking and suckling, Able added, "I'm going to make your body fly."

"I-I—" Olson paused and growled even as he tipped his chin up, offering more room. "I'm not some damn virgin," he grumbled. "No need to be so careful."

Able skimmed his nose along Olson's neck, then bumped under his jaw. "I'm not being careful," he countered before suckling along his jawline, enjoying the slight rasp of whiskers under his tongue. "I'm getting to know my mate, my forever lover."

Olson swallowed so hard his Adam's apple bobbed. "N-No divorce with shifters, eh?"

Lifting his head, Able growled at his mate. "No," he declared. Then, recalling that his wife had left him, Able forced his body to relax. "Once we bond, we won't even want to be apart for great lengths of time." Then Able smirked. "And *I* won't even be able to get it up for another. You're it for me, Olson."

Blowing out a deep breath through pursed lips, Olson swept his gaze over Able's face. He stared at him hard, searching for something, perhaps. A few seconds later, Olson smiled faintly.

"Didn't realize her infidelity had messed me up so bad," Olson whispered. Lifting his hand, he cupped Able's neck. "It was so long ago."

"Healing will take the time it takes," Able replied softly. "But you won't have to worry about that with me."

Olson licked his lips. His gaze strayed to Able's mouth. Then he refocused on his eyes. "Okay."

Able accepted that. Lowering his head, he pressed his lips lightly to Olson's own. Except, his mate was having nothing of that timid crap.

Tightening his grip on Able's neck, Olson tilted his head and nipped at his bottom lip. Able ceded control and opened. Accepting his human's tongue into his mouth, he teased the appendage with his own, lapping and welcoming his invasion.

Olson groaned and tugged his hand free of Able's grip. Wrapping that arm around him, his human pulled him close, flushing their torsos. The move caught Able by surprise, and he lost his balance, flopping half on top of him.

Grunting, Olson turned his head, breaking the kiss. He hissed.

"Damn it," Able snapped, lifting his weight off of Olson. He stared at his human's brown skin, rubbing lightly down his ribs. "How bad is it?"

"It'll pass," Olson assured, not truly answering. He used his grip on Able's chin to urge his focus up and met his gaze. Olson offered him a crooked smile. "If a kiss can do that to me, make me forget all my aches and pains, I can't help but wonder what actual fucking will do."

Able let go of his concern and smiled back at Olson. "How about I take these jeans off you, suck your dick while I open you up, and we'll find out?"

Olson licked his bottom lip before mumbling, "I can't believe I'm considering this. We just met, and our worlds are in upheaval."

"We didn't just meet," Able countered, shaking his head. "We've been interacting for weeks. Our connection started long ago."

Smiling a bit, Olson admitted, "Still coming to grips with that, too, but I'll get there." Then he inhaled deeply only to exhale again. "Use plenty of lube. I only saw part of that monster you're packin', and I know I'm gonna need it."

Heat and need slammed through Able like a flash fire in a pan. "Oh, my mate," he said on a groan. "Never thought I'd get this chance."

Levering to his knees, Able pushed the blanket off of Olson. He scooted backward and reached for his mate's boot laces. As he pulled them off and set them aside, followed by his socks, the scent of tension caught his attention.

The way Olson's abdominals fluttered, clenching and releasing, as well as the way his fingers twitched also betrayed his nerves.

Not wanting to call attention to it, Able vowed to send his

mate soaring. He rubbed up Olson's calves, then his thighs, up to his groin. Even while clearly nervous, Olson still sported a very nicely defined erection behind his fly.

Able popped open Olson's button, then eased down his fly. Admiring the erection outlined in black cotton, he hummed appreciatively. His mouth watered, and he couldn't wait for a taste.

Leaning down, Able pressed his nose between the flaps and inhaled deeply. He moaned out the breath, reveling in the masculine goodness that was his mate's arousal. Opening his mouth, he worked Olson's erection through the material of his underwear, relishing the soft grunts and groans escaping the man. At the same time, Able began working the jeans beneath Olson's globes and down his thighs.

Once Able had the jeans halfway down Olson's powerful thighs, he lifted his head. He held his mate's gaze, pleased to see the glazedness of his eyes, and dipped his fingertips inside the band of the briefs. With a wicked grin, Able eased the band over his cock head, down further, and nuzzled them up under his balls.

Hearing Olson's breathing hitch, seeing the bead of precum bubble up from his mate's slit, Able felt his mouth water. He didn't deny himself.

Able opened his mouth and wrapped his lips around Olson's swollen flesh. When his mate's flavor hit his tongue, it was Able's turn to moan.

Chapter Six

Olson growled under his breath, shuddering hard upon feeling the sweet, wet suction surround his cock. Staring at Able, even knowing the man was turning his world upside down, he couldn't resist what he was offering. As Able worked his cock and balls with mouth and hands, Olson didn't even care that he would end up with a dick in his ass.

Hell, I didn't have a life, anyway.

Pushing those thoughts aside, Olson reached down and threaded his fingers through Able's hair. He enjoyed the feel of the silky strands almost as much as needing the touch to ground him. His balls already felt so sensitive, so tight, that he feared he would pop off after only a minute.

God damn, it's been way too long.

"Able," Olson growled in warning. "Too close."

When Able popped off his dick, Olson groaned in dismay. His new lover winked before reaching over and grabbing something under the corner of the blanket. Seeing that it was lube, Olson felt his chute clench.

"Oh, shit," Olson muttered, unable to help himself. "I'm really doing this."

Able snapped his attention from Olson's groin to his face. Maybe reading his trepidation, he softly told him, "If you want to wait, we can." He rubbed over Olson's hip, teasing into the groove of his groin. "I would never force you. We could start just by rubbing off."

As much as Olson appreciated Able's understanding, he shook his head. "No. You're gonna fuck me and bond us," he declared. "If I'm gonna do this, I'm gonna go all in."

Olson refused to second-guess himself after having made a decision.

For a few seconds, Able stared down at him. His gaze roved over Olson's face, down his torso to his groin, then back to his face. He tilted his head and smiled hungrily. At the same time, Able teased the backs of his forefingers up the length of his still-hard dick.

Narrowing his eyes, Olson ordered, "Now get your mouth back on my cock and open up my ass."

"Yes, my mate," Able purred, using a thumb to open the flip-top of the tube. After pouring a liberal amount onto the fingers of his right hand, Able used that same thumb to close it before tossing it to the left. He rested his now-free hand on Olson's side and rubbed down his body to his hip. "Gods, you're so fucking sexy."

Olson felt his nipples bead at the appreciative touch. His gut clenched as he watched Able lower his slicked fingers between his legs. He did his best not to clench, but he couldn't stop the flinch upon feeling that first touch to his anus.

"Oh, my mate," Able murmured, lowering his head. He nuzzled his cheek along Olson's length. "Let me help you relax."

"Yes, please," Olson mumbled back, completely needing the distraction.

To Olson's relief, Able gave it to him. He opened his mouth and began suckling on the sensitive wrinkled skin beneath his crown. The move sent a spark of heat down his dick, straight to his balls.

"Yessss," Olson hissed, spreading his legs wider and planting his feet. "More."

Able gave it to him. While teasing his balls with his thumb, he massaged his opening, too. With the hand on Olson's hip, Able scraped along the base of his erection, stimulating his sensitive groin skin.

Amidst all that, Able somehow managed to have enough coordination to dip a finger past his guardian muscle. The play distracted Olson enough that his body never felt the need to tense up. He realized exactly how accomplished his lover was and would have felt jealousy, except, in the next instant, Able eased his digit in enough to lightly rub his prostate.

Fire of a different nature shot through his groin. His cock flexed, and his balls tightened. Another touch to the gland tore a groan from his throat as he gripped the blanket beneath him tightly.

Never in Olson's many physicals, where the doctor told him *you're not as young as you used to be*, had it felt like this.

Probably a good thing.

"More," Olson pleaded, his need to feel more outweighing his embarrassment at begging. "God, I need more."

"Anything you want, Olson," Able rumbled, continuing to nuzzle Olson's cock while he spoke. "I'll take care of you."

Then Able swallowed Olson's erection to the root. Moaning, when his lover tried to lift off, sucking strongly, Olson tried to buck back into the exquisite heat of his mouth. Able's hand on his hip held him still, staying his action.

Olson groaned in pleasure and frustration. No one had ever manhandled him before. He didn't know if he hated it or loved it.

Maybe a bit of both.

To Olson's relief, Able quickly sank back down. He lodged Olson's crown in the back of his throat and swallowed. The sweet stimulation nearly sent him over the edge, his orgasm held at bay only by the slight pinch of his ass as Able pushed a second finger into his body.

For the next several minutes, Olson lost himself in Able's ministrations. He would bring him so close to the edge, then take advantage of his delirium to add another finger to his chute. The yo-yo on his body's stimulation caused Olson's mind to nearly float with ecstasy. It was almost better than an orgasm itself.

Then, suddenly, Olson was there. His release shot fire through his veins, and his senses reeled. He moaned Able's name as his lover continued to suck on him, swallowing everything his balls could give him.

Olson felt Able's fingers continue to massage his prostate, prolonging his pleasure. His mind floated with the bliss of it all, and it wasn't until Able eased off his prick that he noticed he hadn't softened one iota. He groaned softly as he peeled open eyelids he didn't remember closing.

Able levered over him, his hazel eyes blazing with need. As soon as his lover realized he stared back at him, the shifter whispered, "First time is easier on your stomach." Able hesitated a second before adding, "But I wanted it to be your choice."

Seeing the way Able eyed him, with a mixture of need and patience, Olson made a snap decision. "I didn't get enough of kissing you earlier." He reached up and wrapped his arms around the other man's shoulders. "Like this. Come here."

Upon hearing Able's rough moan, Olson knew he'd made the right choice. His shifter covered him, reaching between them with one hand. He rested his weight on his other forearm while teasing his fingers into Olson's hair.

"Olson, my mate," Able groaned. "Finally. All mine."

Olson felt Able's cock head bump his opening. He rubbed up and down his lover's back, finding him to be trembling. An urge to reassure filled him, strange and unexpected.

"Oh, Able," Olson murmured into Able's ear. "Take me. Make me yours."

"Yessss," Able hissed.

Feeling the pressure increase against his hole, Olson recalled a bit of advice he'd always thought was odd—push out. When he obeyed, his lover's prick easily slipped past his guardian muscle. The stretch still surprised him, even after feeling Able's fingers inside him. It took every ounce of self-control he had left to keep from clenching.

"That's the way," Able encouraged, mouthing kisses up his neck. "Let me in, my mate. Let me please you."

Olson wasn't certain what else Able expected him to do . . . until he recalled the few times he'd found a twinky little bottom boy to fuck. The young man had always arched his back and pushed into him, welcoming him and encouraging him with his body. While he'd always taken those strangers from behind, Olson figured the premise couldn't be too different.

Gripping tightly to Able's back, Olson used his planted feet to rock into his lover's thrust. He felt his shifter's thick prick sink in deeper, stop, and reverse a little. Keeping his breathing even, he eased back and repeated when Able started pressing again.

Then Olson murmured, "Take me, Able." He threaded his fingers through the other man's hair and tugged lightly, drawing his head down so he could whisper into his ear. "Sink deep. Feel me cradling you."

As Able obeyed, moaning roughly, Olson turned his head and took his lover's lips. He thrust in his tongue, tasting him. His masculine flavor burst across his tongue, tantalizing his taste buds.

Olson lapped at Able's tongue and teased along his teeth. His grip tightened in his lover's hair as he continued to fight for dominance. He relished the dance of tongue and teeth.

When Olson's lungs screamed, he turned his head and groaned. Able's cock pressed against his prostate, rubbing ever-so-lightly as his lover rutted just a smidge. To his shock, his balls were already tight, and his cock ached where it rubbed between them.

Able lifted his head and peered down at him. While holding his gaze with intensity in his eyes, the shifter lifted a finger to play around his lips.

"Sinfully delicious," Able whispered huskily. "Absolutely delicious."

Feeling Able's continued micro-ruts, Olson groaned. He shifted his hips, trying to rock into them, searching for more. His entire body felt strung tight, and his nipples were beaded. Olson knew that if he just had a little bit more . . . something . . . he would be able to come again.

Discovering Able pressed his hips too tightly against his groin, Olson groaned with frustration, unable to move. He dug his fingers into the other man's shoulder blade while gripping his hair tighter. Pulling his lover's face closer, he pinned his lover with a feral grin.

"Fuck me, Able," Olson demanded. "Give us what we both need."

Able opened his mouth on a whine, it sounding suspiciously like a feline yowl. Then . . . he obeyed. Able tucked his head into the crook of Olson's shoulder as he eased his cock most of the way out, only to slam it forward again . . . nailing his prostate in the process.

Olson groaned loudly, shuddering beneath him as blissful fire erupted throughout his body. "Yessss," he snarled, reveling in the hard fucks Able pounded into him, creating powerful shocks to course through him. "That's it." Olson's balls pulled tight so much faster than he would ever have imagined, and his release burst through him once more. "Fuck!"

"Yessss," Able hissed into his ear. "That's it." He continued to saw in and out of Olson's hole, pegging his gland and extending his pleasure. "Milk my cock for my seed."

Even if Olson had wanted to resist — which he didn't — he couldn't. His body felt wrung out beyond his control. He shuddered and jolted, twitched and shivered, beyond anything he could have possibly imagined.

"Olson!"

Able crying his name was the only warning he received. In the next instant, sharp canines sank deep into the crook of Olson's shoulder. He gasped at the pain, then moaned as it morphed into the most erotic sensation.

His nipples tightened, and his gut clenched. From out of nowhere, a third orgasm blindsided him. Barking Able's name, he fell head over heels into bliss. Black spots danced across his vision, and he panted harshly as he floated in ecstasy.

Feeling a lethargy Olson had never before experienced, he grinned loopily up at the ceiling of the tent. He couldn't help but pet the broad shoulders of the man who'd just rocked his world. Even the odd feeling of Able pulling his teeth from his neck—and his prick from his ass—couldn't wipe his smile away.

Easing sideways, Able lay next to Olson. He continued to grip him tightly, as if he feared that if he let go, Olson would disappear.

"Thank you."

Upon hearing Able's whispered words, Olson turned his head and smiled at him. "You just got me off three times, and I'm already forty-two." He snorted as he widened his lips into a grin. "That shouldn't be possible for me anymore."

"It will be with a shifter!"

Olson tensed upon hearing Payson's voice on the other side of the canvas.

The odd man didn't stop there, adding, "Congratulations, kitty!"

Able lifted his head and growled, "Get lost, Payson."

The man cackled even as Kontra's deep voice called, "Leave them alone, Payson."

"Yes, boss."

"Sorry about that," Able mumbled, appearing totally chagrined.

Shrugging one shoulder, Olson pointed out, "We just fucked in a tent in the middle of a campground. I've heard worse from the guys I was with in the military when they wanted to razz someone."

Appearing relieved, Able relaxed back beside Olson. "At least someone can get that crazy hyena to obey."

Olson didn't comment, not entirely certain he thought Able was right.

CHAPTER SEVEN

"I'm sorry to disturb you, Able, but I need to talk to you."

The sound of Alpha Kontra's deep voice outside his tent pulled Able from a light doze. He lifted his head from his pillow and glanced behind him. At some point during the night, he'd ended up the little spoon, with Olson curled up behind him.

Able smiled, liking that his mate wanted to hold him. "Just a minute, Alpha," he replied in a whisper, knowing the shifter's sensitive hearing would allow him to make out his words.

The sound of boots on grass told Able that Kontra was moving away.

"What do you think he wants?"

Hearing Olson's quietly spoken question told Able his mate was awake. "Not sure," he admitted. "Guess I better go see."

"I'll go with you," Olson told him, pushing their blanket down and reaching for his pants in one quick move.

Even as Able admired Olson's smooth dark skin, he gripped his wrist and told him, "You can sleep in if you want. I know you're not a fan of mornings." After cleaning up from their claiming, Able and Olson had finished up their food while sharing more about each other and what their lives had been. Olson had told him that, after getting out of the military, he'd relished every opportunity to sleep in.

Olson dropped his jeans, and at first, Able thought he would take him up on the offer. Instead, he rested his free hand over where Able held his wrist. He smiled and squeezed.

"You remember last night when we got up to piss before going to bed, and you didn't want to let me out of your sight?"

Still a little embarrassed on insisting that he at least be able to see Olson's outline when he stood amidst the dark trees to relieve his bladder, he grimaced. "Yeah."

"You said your cat's instincts, as irrational as it was, told you that I was going to disappear on you?" Olson pressed.

Sighing, Able muttered, "Sorry about that."

Olson shook his head, squeezing his wrist once. "Don't be." Holding Able's gaze in the dim light that managed to filter into the tent, his mate smiled at him. "I feel the same way. You're not going anywhere without me." Then Olson winked and added, "Besides, I smell bacon."

Relief filled Able that his mate understood. "Thank you."

After dipping his chin in a nod, Olson released him and grabbed his jeans once more.

Able quickly followed suit. He picked up a pair of borrowed jeans—from the scent, they were Mutegi's—a large warthog shifter and a pack enforcer. Seeing as the guys didn't know what his frame would be until after he'd shifted, they hadn't been able to get him clothes while buying him a tent.

When Able grabbed the shirt, he guessed it had been Mutegi's, too. He figured if he had to use another's clothes, at least the male's human mate wouldn't be able to scent it, being that he was a human named Ben.

At least it's not Payson's.

Able would rather walk around nude than smell like the damn hyena all the time. Even as he pulled on a pair of socks and boots, he knew he shouldn't be thinking something so uncharitable. All the guys had been super kind and helpful.

He supposed he just didn't like how the hyena didn't listen to anyone but Kontra. Even their beta, a huge Texas longhorn bull shifter—Sam Abbott—didn't bother trying to order the hyena about.

Once dressed, Able led the way out of the tent. He glanced around the campground, taking in the many campsites in the dim pre-dawn light. He spotted over a dozen men already up and moving around. Seven fires had already been started, and a few of them did indeed have the promised bacon sizzling in a pan over them.

Spotting Kontra standing by a fire to the left, Able headed that way. He practically felt Olson flanking his left. His cat appreciated that his mate stayed close.

Kontra turned and faced them, dipping his chin in a nod. "Sorry to wake you so early," he began. Pointing at the kettle resting on a rock ringing the fire, he asked, "Coffee?"

"Yes, please," Olson responded, sounding grateful.

Able shook his head. "No, thank you. I'll take tea if you have it, water if you don't."

"Not just your cat that doesn't like coffee, then?" Kontra asked, his lips twitching. As Able shrugged and shook again, the alpha touched his mate, Tim's, shoulder, and asked, "Is that why you had Yuma grab a box of assorted tea bags on our last grocery run?"

Tim smiled over his shoulder at Kontra. "Of course." Then the oddly scented male reached for a nearby saddlebag.

Even as Able cast a questioning look Kontra's way, he noted how Olson made his coffee—a dash of creamer with a spoonful of sugar. Just because he didn't care for the stuff didn't mean he wouldn't take care of his mate.

"My mate is a warlock," Kontra revealed. "He has visions and can cast spells." With a smirk, he added, "How do you think we took out the facility without any casualties to us?"

"Oh, damn." Able peered at Tim with new respect. "That's amazing."

Tim grinned as he handed over an unopened box of tea bags as well as a tin cup. "It does come in handy from time to time," he told Able with a wink.

"Thank you."

Able took the items, tucking the mug under his arm so he could open the package. After shoving the wrapper into his pocket, he opened the box and chose an orange-flavored black tea. Then he tried to give the box back.

"Keep it," Kontra urged. "Not too many others here would be interested in it."

Nodding, Able repeated, "Thank you." Then he set the box on a nearby chair. He opened his tea bag and placed it in the cup. Turning back to the fire, he saw Olson holding up the canister.

"It's water," Olson told him. Glancing to the left, he told him, "The coffee is instant."

"Oh." Able held up his metal mug as he followed Olson's line of sight. True enough, a metal canister marked with some coffee label he didn't recognize—not that he knew many of them—rested in a cup holder of a folding chair. The fragrance of orange drew his focus back to his mug. Once again, Able found himself thanking someone.

"I need to know everything you both know about Chase Ingerson and the people he works for," Kontra stated after Able had swallowed his first sip of tea.

"Chase Ingerson," Able repeated, seeing as Olson still had his mug to his lips. His eyes were closed, and he looked way too happy to be drinking instant sludge. He fought his urge to smirk and roll his eyes, asking, "Is that the same Chase that was chasing Olson yesterday?"

Kontra nodded. "It is."

"He was one of the elite guards at the facility where I worked," Olson stated, since he'd swallowed his coffee. "I guess he was on vacation when you all took out the facility." Shrugging, he added, "I don't know anything about these other people he's working for, though."

A muscle flexed in Kontra's jaw before he growled, "Well, the asshole's good. I'll give him that." Crossing his arms over his chest, his coffee mug held in his front hand, Kontra stated, "He escaped during the night. Must have had a knife hidden somewhere that we didn't find. Payson followed his trail for three miles to a gas station. Payson arrived just in time to see him step away from a phone booth and get into a black, unmarked SUV." Glancing between them, Kontra continued, "Payson found Chase's scent on the phone, but when we tried to redial, it went directly to an automated response that wanted an extension. I have Lamar looking into it."

"Shit," Olson rumbled. "How long ago was that?"

"Half an hour ago," Kontra replied before taking another sip of his coffee.

"We need to get out of here," Able whispered, looking at Olson. "They'll be coming for you." He glanced around, noticing the increase in activity. "After all of us."

"We're prepping to leave, but we have a little time. We didn't bring him to our campground." Kontra pointed to the south. "A couple of miles south, though, so we shouldn't be too hard to find," the bear shifter admitted before taking a plate of bacon, eggs, and hash browns from Tim, thanking his mate, who held a plate for himself. "But we're not leaving just yet. I want to see who comes looking for us."

"You'd put your own mate in danger to—" Able began, shocked, then spotted Kontra's quelling look and snapped his mouth shut.

"Make no mistake, Able," Kontra began gruffly. "We are *more* than capable of taking out a bunch of human soldiers." Then his eyes narrowed as he added, "And we need more men to question so we can clear out more facilities." Kontra's dark eyes glimmered with malice. "It's time these stooges were wiped out, once and for all, and I mean to make it my mission in life to do just that." Waving a hand at the men

49

around him, Kontra added, "All my people are in. If you don't want to help, I'll send you somewhere safe."

Able opened his mouth, more than ready to take that option to get his mate away from those who hunted them both.

"I'd like to help," Olson stated, gripping Able's elbow in a light hold to catch his attention. "There's no telling how many of your kind died while I was working at the facility. This is a way for me to atone."

Before Able could counter him, Tim did. "There's nothing for you to atone for." The sandy-blond-haired man shrugged. "You can't fix something if you don't know it's broken."

Yuma approached, holding out a pair of plates to both Olson and Able. "Exactly. I mean, help is always welcome, and we all have our jobs." After they'd taken the plates, Yuma smirked as he waved at his lithe, five-foot-seven-inch body. "I don't fight, but I help in the background. Hence, food." Then Yuma winked and sashayed away.

Able really wanted to deny Olson, but he couldn't. If his mate pressed his desire, Able would be right there with him. He ground his teeth for an instant, then glanced between Olson and Kontra. "I'll follow where my mate leads," he announced before focusing on Olson. "But they're right. You didn't know that what was going on there was wrong. This shouldn't fall on your conscience."

Olson scoffed softly. Holding a piece of bacon between his thumb and forefinger, he stared at it. "I almost called an anonymous tip in to some random environmentalist group on so many occasions." He met Able's gaze. "Now, I wish I had. My instincts were right that the place was shady." With a bitter smile, Olson added, "That's what I'll have to live with."

Ryan appeared, stopping beside them. "I helped them, too, Olson." His eyes narrowed as he cocked his head. "I understand where you're coming from, but believe me, looking back on *what ifs* will not help your conscience."

Olson smiled and nodded. "You're right." His expression turned into a hard grin. "All you can do is move forward." He focused on Able, holding his gaze steadily. "If I'm going to be part of your world, then I need to start somewhere." Glancing around, Olson narrowed his eyes and murmured, "And this is a great place to start." He returned his focus to Able. "Can we do that, my mate?"

A shiver went down Able's spine upon hearing Olson calling him mate. To hear that, he would have done damn near anything.

Smiling warmly at Olson, Able told him, "I'll help you do anything, Olson. Anything at all."

CHAPTER EIGHT

Olson knew Able's instinct had been to flee. He also appreciated that, for Olson's sake, he hadn't pressed the issue. Instead, Able stood at Olson's side as the group talked about what Lamar had found.

"You worked for a company called Winter Heights Pharmaceuticals," Lamar told him. His voice turned hard. "They say they're researching a cure for Parkinson's, not that any of their research was actually on the disease. That was totally a cover." Frowning at his tablet, Lamar added, "They're a satellite company for a pharmaceutical company, The Burgess Foundation, funded by a bunch of anonymous donors."

"Does The Burgess Foundation have any other satellite companies?" Adam asked, frowning. "And where is its headquarters?" He cracked his knuckles and chuckled. "We should pay them a visit."

Adam's mate, Noah, stared fondly at the white tiger shifter, even as he shook his head. Noah's younger brother, Ronnie, smirked at Adam and crossed his arms over his brawny chest. Both men were moose shifters, and even though Ronnie was only twenty-two, he was far larger and more dominant.

Olson had heard that was one of the reasons they'd left their moose herd. Even by eighteen, Ronnie's moose had been having a hard time submitting to their alpha, who happened to be their sister's mate. It had created a bit of friction in the family. Adam had taken them both to Kontra and their gang, who he'd ridden with for decades before meeting and mating with Noah.

All Olson cared about was the fact he'd heard they were all good in a fight. In fact, everyone in Kontra's gang seemed to function as a well-oiled machine. He'd heard that their base group, a dozen shifters of various animals, had been riding together for almost thirty years before the first had found his mate, giving the rest of them hope to keep looking.

Evidently, they'd all eventually found their mates, then started adding more members and helping them to do the same.

"They're right here in Louisiana," Lamar answered Adam's question. His blue eyes gleamed with anger as he added, "And they're only thirty miles east of here."

"Ironic that, if they hadn't tried to go after you, Olson, they wouldn't even be on our radar," Sam commented. The scar on the big, dark-haired beta's cheek crinkled oddly as he smirked. "Now we'll shut them down sooner rather than later."

"All in good time." Kontra pointed at Lamar. "Keep going. How many facilities are we looking at?"

"According to The Foundation's records, eight," Lamar revealed with a grimace. "And they're not just in this country."

Eli grumbled, "Of course, they're not."

The doctor's little wolf shifter mate, also named Sam, sighed and leaned into the other man. "I'm tired of these guys already."

"So's the Shifter Council," Kontra revealed, a wicked grin curving his lips as a feral gleam entered his brown eyes. "After we kick the ass of anyone who comes looking for us here, we're going to take out the headquarters." Glancing around at his people, Kontra added, "We may end up getting help from others, but the Shifter Council is working with the Vampire Councils, here and overseas, so we can hit all of them at the same time." Pleasure filled his voice. "They'll never know what hit them."

Olson prayed the plan worked, but something he'd learned early in the military was that even the best-laid plans could easily go awry.

"So, when do we expect our visitors?" Grimes asked. He was a lion shifter. "Any idea how many we're expecting?"

Upon learning how many different species made up Kontra's pack, Olson had been blown away at the diversity. He'd heard the term menagerie once and completely thought it appropriate. Especially considering, the shifters they'd rescued from the facility where Able had been had all been different, too—including a panda bear, a rhino, a meerkat, a vulture, and a sloth.

Several of Kontra's men had taken them to a hotel thirty miles in the opposite direction to keep them safe. A number of guards were included in that group as well as smaller members who either didn't have the training to fight or were too timid to do so.

That still left over a dozen men—shifter, human, vampire, warlock, and even fae—Olson had had a hard time understanding that one until Elron lowered his glamour and showed his true form, complete with lavender eyes and pointed ears.

"I heard from Mutegi a few minutes before we started this meeting," Kontra revealed. "There are three SUVs, and each can carry seven men, so we should expect at least that many, and if they maintain a steady pace and don't have too much trouble finding us, they'll be here within the hour." Surveying his group, the alpha reminded, "Their tranqs will take you down, so do your best to avoid giving them a shot. Our warlocks will cast spells to cause their darts to go awry, but don't rely too heavily on them, since there could be too many." Lifting his hands, Kontra added, "And as always, these men are this company's elite, which means they'll most likely be enhanced in some way. Don't expect them to fight like a human would." He smirked and eyed Olson. "No offense."

Olson couldn't help the way his lips twitched. "None taken."

"Okay." Kontra started talking again. "Here's how I want to see this go." Then he laid out a plan.

Twenty minutes later, Olson sat next to the fire, a cup of coffee in hand. He gripped it tightly between his palms as he stared at Kontra, who was seated to his left. Olson hated that he'd been separated from Able, but he understood the tactic.

Those shifters who could use the trees for cover had been ordered to hide in the branches and take out any guards who were easy pickings . . . or to protect them from a second wave.

Eli hadn't been any happier about it than Olson, since it meant the doctor would be in anaconda form in a tree, while Sam remained in camp in human form. Still, after a deep kiss, the doctor had headed into the woods. Many of the mated shifters had ended up needing to split up, including the beta's human, Ryan, who was a sniper by training. He'd headed into the trees, too.

Grimes had as well, even though a lion wasn't the greatest at climbing trees. Due to his human brain, he could. Fortunately for Grimes, his bobcat mate, Chip, was at the hotel with those who'd been rescued.

"Try to stay calm, Olson," Elron urged with a confident smile. He relaxed in his chair. "We're good at this."

Olson tried to emulate the fae, relaxing back in his chair. "Not so easy to do when I know they can all kick my ass," he admitted before lifting his mug to his lips. The coffee wasn't great, but he would take it.

"Don't be so sure," Ronnie rumbled from Olson's right. On his other side sat Hector, Ronnie's armadillo mate, and they held hands. "I hear humans gain their gifts swiftly, especially when under duress."

Before Olson could come up with a response, the loud caw of a crow sounded overhead. He looked up, spotting Castor, Elron's shifter mate. The crow winged over their campsites—only five appeared to be occupied—and landed in the boughs of a cypress tree.

"Castor says one SUV is turning into the campground," Elron told them. "The other pair stopped half a mile away, and fourteen men and women are headed your way, skirting a swamp." He cocked his head and asked, "Really?" Then Elron grinned. "He says one has already been bitten by a water moccasin. Even if he survives, it'll sure slow him down."

Olson had been blown away when he'd learned that vampires and fae would develop mind-links with their partners, allowing them to speak telepathically.

There's just so damn much to learn.

"Get ready, gentlemen," Kontra called to those around other campfires.

As I'll ever be. Olson didn't voice the comment.

Hearing the rumble of an engine, Olson turned his head and watched the SUV stop, blocking in a number of *Harleys*. The doors opened, and seven people—five men and two women—poured from the vehicle. They already had guns in hand.

Olson focused on Chase, who smirked at him.

"Well done, Chase," the man who'd exited from the front passenger seat commented. "Not only do we get the traitor, but we get his associates as well."

"Happy to help, General Farthing," Chase replied. Pointing his gun at Olson, he told him, "Told you I knew you were lying. I can't wait to see what experiments the scientists cook up on your friends, here." He stretched out his arm and added, "But you're no longer of use." Then Chase fired his gun.

The loud bang revealed it was not a tranquilizer gun.

Olson's heart nearly stopped in his chest, fearing he'd made a life-ending mistake. Except, the bullet pinged off some invisible shield, as if it were hitting metal, and ricocheted back toward the SUV. All the guards hit the dirt, several issuing a cry of surprise.

"What the hell?" Chase growled, rising to his knees.

"They must have witches hiding in the woods," General Farthing guessed, obviously having more knowledge of the paranormal world than at least some of the others. He pointed at the pair to the far left. "Fire the anti-magick grenade."

The pair rushed to the back of the SUV and began grabbing something from the back.

Olson looked at Kontra, who still sat reclining in his chair. The big man peered at Elron. "Anti-magick gun? Think it works on your kind?"

Elron shrugged. "I'll let you know after they fire it."

"Shouldn't you try to stop them?" Olson demanded, shocked that none of the guys were trying. In fact the only movement came from the men at the other fires, who were creeping closer.

"I can't wait to make you smug bastards squirm like a worm on a hook," the general continued as he sneered at them. "You don't belong on this earth, and soon we'll eradicate all of you."

"Relax, Olson," Kontra replied with a smile. "We'll be fine."

Before Kontra had even finished speaking, two shots fired in rapid succession. A slug hole appeared in the head of each man assembling the weapons—one in a guy's temple, the other in his forehead. Both men dropped.

"See." Kontra winked. Then he rose from his camp chair. "So, gentlemen, shall we try this again?" He wedged his coffee cup into the folding chair's holder and crossed his arms over his chest. "Why are you attacking my friends and forcing us to defend ourselves?"

Instead of answering Kontra, General Farthing lifted his wrist to his mouth and spoke. "Attack." Then he ducked behind the SUV along with Chase and the other men.

To Olson's surprise, nothing happened.

General Farthing must have been shocked, too, because he lifted his wrist to his mouth again and yelled, "I said, Attack!"

Still nothing.

A pale man in a black cloak rode through what looked like a portal, appearing between one instant and the next. "Sorry to interrupt." He stopped his pale horse off to the side, forming a triangle between himself, the SUV, and the campfire. Focusing on the general, he tapped his thin forefinger on the shaft of the scythe he carried and stated, "General Farthing, your men are no longer available. Please tell me how you know about witches."

"Who the fuck are you?" the general screamed right before he fired his gun at the figure.

With a swish of his scythe, the male deflected the bullet. "I am the Horseman of Death, Dodge Farthing, and I asked you a question."

CHAPTER NINE

A ble stared at the winged creatures below him, tension fill-
ing him. While he'd never seen anything like them, he
could guess at what they were — demons. He just didn't know
what they were doing there.

As Able watched, a demon appeared behind each of the
soldiers. Each of them were black as night, but they varied a
smidge in size and shape, too. Some had fully formed wings,
while others didn't appear to have the ability to fly on their
appendages.

Each seized one of the creeping guards, easily disarming
them. Then they whispered a few words while touching the
human's temples, causing them to drop. The demons caught
the attackers and slung them over their shoulders before start-
ing toward the campground.

One demon stopped and tipped his head up, sweeping his
gaze over the tree where Able hid. He met his gaze and
grinned. "Hello, Able Lieder, all these humans have been
neutralized. You may return to the campground and your
mate."

Even in cat form, Able couldn't help but gape. He watched
in shock as the demon continued walking. Unable to contain
his curiosity, he turned and followed the demon, jumping
from branch to branch, staying in the trees.

When the cypress trees gave way to a bit of space where
the campgrounds were located, Able paused and peered
around the area. An SUV blocked in a couple of *Harleys*, in-

cluding Kontra's hog. A man with long white hair and aristocratic features, dressed in a black cloak, sat atop a horse, his attention focused on the figures hiding behind the vehicle—three men and two women.

The demons exited the trees and, one by one, laid out their sleeping or unconscious cargo. Then they took a step back and crossed their arms over their chests.

"That's all of them," a huge black male with massive wings stated.

"Thank you, Bal," the strange rider stated, a pleased smile curving his lips as he glanced the demon's way. "I can always count on you, my general."

Bal dipped his head, saying, "It's always an honor to serve you, Master Death."

That was when it clicked.

Death. Horseman of the Apocalypse. What the hell is he doing here?

"Horseman of Death," Kontra spoke up, dipping his head in deference. "Thank you for your assistance."

Payson, naked as the day he was born, strolled into view. "Even if it did make life a little anti-climactic." A wide grin spread across his lips. "Hey, Balthazar. Good to see you again, demon." As Payson walked past the demon, he held out his fist, clearly expecting the huge male to bump it.

"Interesting to see so much of you," Balthazar replied, but he did bump Payson's fist.

Laughing, Payson gripped his soft prick. "You're just enjoyin' the view."

Shaking his head, Balthazar told him bluntly, "I'm actually wondering how Peter would respond if I had a Jacob's Ladder combined with my *lackchet*."

Payson laughed. "You should ask him. Maybe he'll want to find out."

While Able knew the Jacob's Ladder was the small piercings running up Payson's dick, he had no idea what a *lackchet* was.

Must be a demon thing.

"I would prefer anti-climactic when it keeps all of us safe," Kontra countered. Then he focused on Death once more. "Is there some way we may be of assistance to you" — then he smiled and waved toward the three men and two women still hiding behind the SUV — "after we deal with these guys."

"Indeed there is, Alpha Kontra," Death stated with a smile. Then he turned his attention to the five figures and the SUV. "You have not answered my question, General Farthing. How do you know about witches?"

"I'm not answering any of your questions," one of the men answered — General Farthing, evidently. He pulled a cross from his pocket and held it before him. "Release my people and leave this plane, demon. I banish you from —"

Laughter erupted from the over a dozen demons standing around, causing the general to pause.

"Does he really think that will work?" Payson asked with a snort. He shook his head as he added, "So, how do you want to take them out?"

Kontra shrugged. "I don't think we'll have to." Tipping his chin toward the demons, he indicated their actions.

The black figures leaped into the sky and flew over the SUV.

The general stumbled backward, clearly not expecting the move. Three of his followers started firing into the sky at the creatures. The final man shoved the general toward Death, then rushed at Kontra.

"This is all your fault, traitor!" the man screamed, and Able realized that human had to be Chase . . . and he was rushing at Olson.

Snarling in rage, Able lunged from the tree and bounded across the small clearing. Except, he wasn't fast enough. Even those standing next to Olson seemed too surprised to act.

Olson, however, had no trouble responding. He side-stepped easily, while sticking out his foot, tripping Chase. The man recovered swiftly and rolled to his back, wielding his gun, pointing it at Olson. Able's mate, swept out his foot, kicking Chase's wrist, sending the gun flying.

When Chase began to rise, Able arrived. He landed his claws on the man's chest while wrapping his jaws around the bastard's throat. Only Olson's hand on his back stayed his desire to tear out the human's throat.

"I would advise you to stay down, Chase," Olson warned. "I won't ask Able to stop a second time."

If looks could kill, they would both have been dead . . . but Chase stayed still.

Balthazar knelt beside them. He touched Chase's temple and whispered a few words. The man's eyes rolled to the back of his head.

As much as it galled him to do it, Able released Chase unharmed.

"Thank you," Olson murmured, rubbing the fur of his back. "I think Death has other ideas for these men."

Able initiated his shift, pleased to find that it no longer hurt to resume his human form. As soon as he could, he stood and wrapped his arms around his mate. Dipping his head, Able captured Olson's lips, thrusting his tongue in deep.

"Oh, yeah." Payson's voice cut into their moment. "Too bad I can't get hard without Land here, or you all would totally be givin' me a boner!"

Ending the kiss, Able glared at the crazy hyena shifter. "Thanks for ruining the moment," he grumbled.

"It's for the best, I'm afraid," Kontra told them, an amused smirk twisting his goateed lips. Able still noticed the alpha kept a tight arm around Tim's waist as he continued, "We have business to attend to before you can get to victory sex. Grab a pair of sweats."

Able wished with all his heart that he could tell the alpha, *You have business to attend to.* He knew when to keep his mouth shut, though, so he didn't. Instead, he murmured, "Yes, Alpha." That didn't stop him from gripping Olson's hand and making certain his mate accompanied him to his tent.

"We'll get to the victory sex later," Olson assured on a whisper.

Noticing Adam's smirk as the tiger shifter yanked on a pair of sweatpants, Able knew his mate's comment hadn't been nearly as quiet as he'd thought it was. He would have to remind his lover of how sensitive a paranormal's hearing was at some point.

Seeing as Able didn't want to embarrass Olson by ignoring the comment — and he had every intention of doing exactly as his mate had said — Able murmured back, "I can hardly wait." His half-hard prick could corroborate his desires.

Able ducked into their tent and grabbed the sweatpants he'd left there. After yanking them on, he accepted the tank top Olson offered him. As he pulled that on, he slid his feet into a pair of sandals.

Bloody hot in Louisiana.

After that, hand-in-hand, Able led Olson back to the gathering group. He noticed that all the attackers had been whisked away, and most of the demons were gone. Balthazar remained as well as two that were just as huge as the six-foot-six demon. Their master, Death, was still there as well.

Once everyone had assembled and found their drink of choice — Able took a glass of wine, while Olson accepted a beer — Kontra rose to his feet. He punched a button on a tablet set up before him. After a distinctive ringing noise, someone answered.

"Hello, Alpha."

"Greetings, Ben," Kontra replied, saying hello to Mutegi's mate, a human who'd gone to the hotel for safety. "Has everyone assembled with you?"

"Yes, Alpha," Ben confirmed. "We're all here."

"Excellent." Kontra lifted the tablet. "I'm going to pass you off to Mutegi."

"Hey, handsome," Ben greeted. "Miss you."

"Miss you, too," the huge African — a warthog shifter — replied, a warm smile curving his full lips as he peered at the screen.

Kontra turned his attention back to the assembled shifters and mates. "Thank you for joining me," he began. "I know each of you would much rather be doing something else after the tension of a battle." Leveling a heated look Tim's way, Kontra added, "I know I certainly would be." Then he used a hand to indicate Death. "However, we have an important visitor, the Horseman of Death, and I imagine he wouldn't come here unless his request wasn't grave." Wincing, Kontra grumbled, "No pun intended."

Payson snickered, and he wasn't the only one.

Even Able had to work hard to keep his lips from twitching.

After shaking his head, Kontra continued, "Death has been gracious enough to remove the threat of General Farthing and his men, and I've explained where they came from." His expression darkened. "It seems there's a bigger issue the general is connected with or has been connected with. A rogue circle of witches," he growled.

Able felt his pulse spike in his chest a little. Shifters and witches historically did not get along. For some reason, they liked to use their animals for gain, which really made no sense to Able.

A glance at Tim and Draven — both warlocks — male magick-users — told Able that they weren't pleased, scowling in anger.

"What do you want, Death?" Payson asked, his tone actually containing concern for once. "Us to go up against them or something?"

"No." Death now stood on the ground, his mount nowhere to be seen. "My brothers and I have already dealt with the circle in question, although we don't know if other circles are involved."

"What do you mean?" Adam piped up. "How could you deal with it and not know if the problem is solved?"

Death fixed a steady gaze on the tiger shifter. "Each circle of witches has a certain magickal signature," Death explained. "My brothers and I ran into a circle helping human hunters attack demons they thought were vampires, and we thought we'd eradicated everyone. We missed one." Turning his head, Death glared over their heads. "We discovered even larger underlying problems, and we're still clearing them up, but we've run into a snag."

Kontra tipped his head a little as he narrowed his eyes. "What kind of snag?" After a second of hesitation, he added, "And not that I'm not grateful that our paths overlap again, but why us?" Pinning a questioning look on Death, Kontra added, "I'm certain it's not by accident."

Dipping his head in acknowledgment, Death admitted, "You're right. I'm not here by chance." Then he scoffed softly, his tone taking on a dark turn. "Although, running into those yahoos was a happy turn of chance." Death smiled in an almost creepy way. "I can't wait to pick those men's brains."

"What will happen to them?"

Able turned toward the tablet screen, not at all surprised to find that it was the kind-hearted Yuma who asked the question.

Death eyed the screen impassively. "That will be decided by the fates."

Chapter Ten

Olson was trying to keep up. Really, he was. His brain still reeled with the knowledge that the Horseman of Death had stepped in to stop the attack. True, he had an ulterior motive, but it still blew his mind.

"If the Moirai tell me their souls are to be harvested, it will be done," Death continued, not showing the least sign of remorse. "They weave the skein of all men's souls."

To Olson, that sounded as if each man had a finite amount of time on the earth. Then he realized that plenty of people thought that was true. When it was their time to die . . . it was, and nothing would change it.

Feeling Able squeeze his hand, Olson glanced his lover's way and smiled before refocusing on Death.

"I came because I have a request," Death revealed, staring steadily at Kontra. "Upon destroying that circle of witches, we discovered they'd used some kind of blood magick to control shifters."

"What?" Kontra snarled, his body tensing. "How is that possible?"

Death lifted his hand in an obvious attempt to placate. "This circle of witches was helping hunters capture and kill our demons. Then they were utilizing demon blood in their spells." Shaking his head, Death admitted, "We're still searching for the source of these spells, something called The Red Book, so if you hear anything of it, please let me know."

Kontra turned his head a little, giving Death a side-eyed look. "And this is why you came here? To ask us to keep our ears open?"

Shaking his head, Death admitted, "No. Five of these mag-icked shifters, all black bears, still live, but are in some kind of . . . trance." He frowned as he rubbed the back of his neck with one long-fingered hand. "We can't even get them to eat unless we physically open their mouths and put food in. Then they'll chew and swallow. We just don't know how to help them." Death lifted his hands, palms up, in a frustrated, help-less gesture. "We're hoping it's just because our magicks aren't compatible." Waving his hand at Tim and Draven, he added, "Demon magick versus magick from this plane."

"And you want us to see if we can figure out a spell to help them?" Draven spoke the question, his pale blue eyes narrow-ing on Death, although he appeared lost in thought. "To find a spell to counter what they did?"

Death nodded once. "I know it's a tall order to ask."

"We can help at least one of them."

Upon hearing Tim's vacant-sounding words, Olson snapped his gaze to Kontra's mate. He gasped upon spotting the slightly glazed expression on his face and how his eye-brows were narrowed. The male appeared to be seeing some-thing no one else could see.

Right . . . visions. Guess that's a real thing.

"Do you see it?" Tim asked, lifting his hand, palm up.

Draven immediately took Tim's hand, and his pale blue eyes turned just as vacant. "Hmmm, interesting." After a few seconds, Draven released Tim's hand and blinked a couple of times. "It's worth a shot."

"What's worth a shot?" Kontra asked warily.

Tim blinked several times as he shook his head. "Still can't seem to get used to that," he mumbled, obviously coming back to himself.

"Babe?" Kontra questioned.

Blowing out a breath, Tim peered up at Kontra. "There's one sure-fire way to break the spell," he revealed. "And that's for the shifter to meet his mate." Then Tim grinned. "And we already have the mate of one of the bears here." Then he furrowed his brows. "Although, I'm not certain which bear it is. We'd have to take them all."

"But . . . how would we take care of them?" Sam asked, pressing into Eli's side. The dark-skinned wolf shifter glanced around at them all. "If they won't respond, how can we find the other mates?"

Tim opened his mouth, only to close it again and shake his head.

Even Draven, who Olson understood was a couple of centuries old and Tim's mentor and teacher, didn't seem to have an answer.

Groaning, Kontra lifted his gaze to the sky. The alpha squinted, then grimaced, as if he were struggling with himself. After several seconds, he slowly panned over the group gathered around him. He even focused on the tablet.

"Did everyone on your end hear all that, Ben?" Kontra called.

After a few seconds of silence, Ben quietly answered, "Yes. We all heard."

Kontra nodded, then swept his gaze over his group again. "I know you all recognize me as your alpha, and for that, I will forever feel honored." After a pause, where he seemed to be struggling with his thoughts, he continued, "Now, we're dealing with magick and enchantments that are beyond a shifters' ability to counter or control." Kontra's gaze fell on Tim and Draven. "Even as we have the opportunity to use them to our advantage, they can be used against us as well . . . and have been, in the past."

Olson glanced around, taking in all the grim faces. Even Payson appeared serious as they all hung on every word the big grizzly shifter uttered.

"Deciding to take out scientists and guards with guns is

one thing, something we can counter with speed, planning, tenacity, and our healing gifts," Kontra stated in his deep booming voice. "Magick is a bit more difficult." He once again glanced at Tim and Draven, even going so far as to thread his fingers through his mate's hair. "Even with our mates at our sides, there's so much we can't control." Lifting his gaze to peer at everyone again, Kontra stated, "You have followed me faithfully, but right now, every one of you must make a choice." His brows furrowed as he ordered, "Talk to your mate. Make your decision. Regardless of whether you follow me or not, you will always be welcome at my campfire." Then Kontra stated calmly, "I will accept these magicked shifters. I will strive to help them, wherever that leads me." Meeting Tim's gaze, who nodded slightly and smiled, "With my mate at my side." The bear shifter again swept his gaze over everyone. "This is a personal decision, so if you need time, I will not begrudge you. I've been honored to ride with you all."

Then, to Olson's surprise, Kontra turned his back on everyone to meet Death's impassive expression. With his arm around Tim's waist, he told the horseman, "Please bring the bears in the morning. I'll find a way to help as many of them as I can."

"It will be so. I'll see you here in the morning." Death dipped his head, then turned away. "I'll leave some of my generals to monitor the area, just in case the Foundation sends reinforcements. You will all be safe." A second later, between one step and the next, Death had disappeared.

Olson glanced around the area as he took in the shifters and humans around him. He expected to see a myriad of expressions . . . but there weren't. Even as they glanced between each other, they appeared more annoyed than anything else.

Finally, Payson snarled and lunged forward. He grabbed Kontra's wrist, staying his retreat to his tent. The alpha half-turned and arched a brow in silent question, and Payson released him to land fisted hands on his hips.

"I've been with ya since you found me hidin' in the woods, starving because I was too afraid of my own shadow to travel more than a mile from my cave," Payson declared, scowling fiercely at Kontra. "You saved me, and I've been followin' you ever since. I've never had cause to regret it." The crazy hyena shifter glanced around at everyone before refocusing on Kontra. "None of us have." Crossing his arms over his chest, Payson stated, "I may be crazy, but I'm pretty damn certain that the only way any of us would have regrets, would be because we walked away from you when we have more shifters to help."

Kontra arched a brow as one side of his goateed lips curved into a smile. "Oh really?"

Payson narrowed his eyes and jerked a nod. "Damn right, *really.*"

Turning fully, Kontra faced the group. He even glanced toward the tablet, which still connected them to Ben and the rest at the motel. His eyes narrowed as he surveyed the group before tipping his head back and sniffing, scenting the wind.

A hint of pleasure seemed to light Kontra's dark eyes. "The rest of you feel that way?"

"Hell, yeah!" nearly everyone cried in unison. Then, pumping their fists in the air, they cried, "Kontra! Kontra! Kontra!"

Feeling his heart thud in his chest, Olson exchanged a glanced with Able, smiled at his lover, then joined in the chant. To his pleasure, his shifter joined right along with him.

Olson didn't miss how Tim bumped Kontra's shoulder and murmured something to him, although he couldn't make out what it was.

Kontra smiled at Tim, then lifted his hands toward the gang. Almost immediately, everyone silenced. The quiet stood testimony to everyone's respect for the huge male.

"Better get some sleep, everyone," Kontra shouted. "There'll be plenty to do tomorrow."

With those parting words, Kontra again turned and headed toward his tent.

As Olson spotted everyone breaking up, some patting him and Able on their shoulders or backs as they passed, he realized he'd just been accepted into a brand-new family. He watched for several seconds, seeing how those who'd put away supplies to make their camp look smaller began to pull things out and set things up. Others stoked fires and started cooking meat. A few even disappeared between the cypress trees.

Grinning broadly, Olson grabbed Able's hand and began leading him toward their tent. "Come on," he urged gruffly, his body thrumming with a new sense of victory. "Time to have that winner's sex we talked about." With another look around, Olson added, "Then we'll help our new family finish whatever tasks they need help with."

Able laughed, seeming to be on board with that. "Sex, then help. Got it."

Olson laughed right along with him as he tumbled his leopard into their tent. Sprawled over Able, taking his mouth in a deep kiss, Olson knew he was more than ready to face whatever uncertain future was heading his way.

ABOUT THE AUTHOR

Charlie started writing fantasy when she was eight, and after stumbling onto her first erotic romance at age nineteen, she realized her true calling. She now focuses on writing gay erotic romance, normally of the paranormal variety, with heroes of all kinds. With the help and support of her husband, Charlie finally fulfilled one of her life-long goals . . . move to acreage with her horses. You can often find her curled up with her laptop and a cup of tea or glass of wine, creating her next adventure. Charlie enjoys exploring the mountains of her new Oregon home on horseback, 4-wheeler, or motorcycle.

She can be reached at ch.richards2010@yahoo.com
Or visit her at www.charlie-richards.com

www.ingramcontent.com/pod-product-compliance
Lightning Source LLC
Chambersburg PA
CBHW071201130626
46555CB00004B/1539